MEGAN AND THE BOREALIS BUTTERFLY
by Nina Alexander

Illustrations by
Dan Burr

Spot Illustrations by
Rich Grote

MAGIC ATTIC PRESS

Published by Magic Attic Press.

For more information contact:
Book Editor, Magic Attic Press, 866 Spring Street,
Westbrook, ME 04092-3808

First Edition
Printed in the United States of America
1 2 3 4 5 6 7 8 9 10

Magic Attic Club® is a registered trademark.

Christine E. Taylor, Publisher
Cindy Lawhorn, Art Director
Debra DeForte, Managing Editor

Edited by Judit Bodnar
Designed by Cindy Lawhorn

Alexander, Nina
Megan and the Borealis Butterfly / by Nina Alexander
Illustrations by Dan Burr, spot illustrations by Rich Grote
(Magic Attic Club)
Summary: When Megan finds herself transported to the Amazon rain forest, she can
hardly believe her eyes! She meets a young girl named Dana who lives there with her
parents. Dana tells Megan about the mysterious Borealis Butterfly and her quest to find it
in the rain forest. Megan eagerly helps her search for the beautiful butterfly until she
learns the *real* reason behind Dana's quest. Can Megan stop her before it's too late?
ISBN 1-57513-153-6 (hardback) ISBN 1-57513-152-8 (paperback)
ISBN 1-57513-154-4 (library edition hardback)

As members of the
MAGIC ATTIC CLUB,
we promise to
be best friends,
share all of our adventures in the attic,
use our imaginations,
have lots of fun together,
and remember—the real magic is in us.

Alison   Keisha

Heather   Megan

Rose

Table of Contents

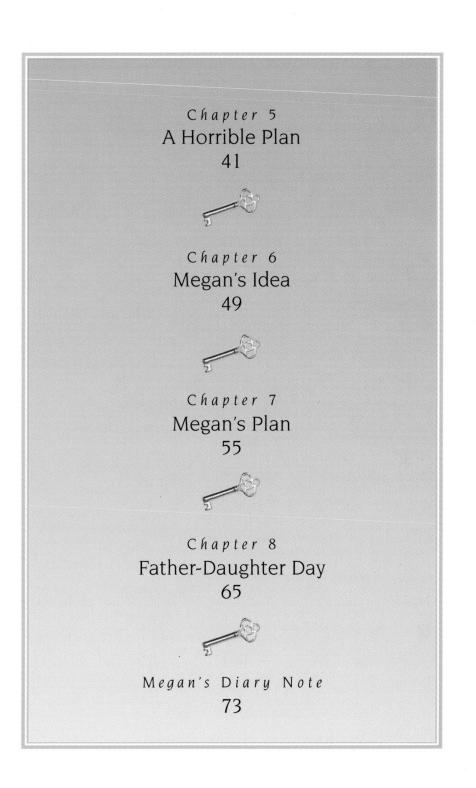

Prologue

When Alison, Heather, Keisha, and Megan find a
golden key buried in the snow, they have no idea that it
will change their lives forever. They discover that it
belongs to Ellie Goodwin, the owner of an old Victorian
house across the street from Alison's. Ellie, grateful when
they return the key to her, invites the girls to play in her
attic. There they find a steamer trunk filled with wonderful
outfits—party dresses, a princess gown, a ballet tutu,
cowgirl clothes, and many, many, more. The girls try on
some of the costumes and admire their reflections in a
tall, gilded mirror nearby. Suddenly they are transported
to a new time and place, embarking on the greatest
adventure of their lives.

After they return to the present and Ellie's attic,
they form the Magic Attic Club, promising to tell
each other every exciting detail of their future
adventures. Then they meet Rose Hopkins, a new
girl at school, and invite her to join the club and
share their amazing secret.

Chapter

One

AN EXCITING
PHONE CALL

egan!" Aunt Frances called from downstairs. "Megan, it's for you!"

Megan Ryder looked up from the book she was reading and blinked in surprise, wondering who could be calling her. Her best friends were supposed to be on their way over to her house right now. She hoped they weren't calling to say they couldn't come.

"Megan!" Aunt Frances called again, louder this time. "Hurry! Your dad's on the phone!"

Megan quickly tossed aside her book. "Coming!" she shouted back.

She hurried out of her bedroom, almost tripping over Ginger, who was sleeping near the door in a patch of warm summer sunlight. "Oops!" she said, jumping over the cat at the last second. "Sorry, Ginger." Ginger didn't even twitch as her owner turned down the hall toward the stairs.

Taking the polished wooden steps two at a time, Megan rushed down to the sunny kitchen. Her aunt stood there holding the phone and smiling.

"That was fast, Megs," Aunt Frances said, handing over the phone. She treated Megan more as if she were a friend or a younger sister than a niece. Megan loved having her around, especially when she wanted to talk with someone.

"Thanks, Aunt Frances," Megan said, panting a little. She took the phone and spoke into it. "Hello? Dad, is that really you? It seems like ages since the last time we talked."

"It's really me." Her father's familiar laugh came through the receiver. "It's only been a little over a week, actually. But it feels like a lot longer to me, too. How's my favorite daughter?"

Megan grinned. "I'm your *only* daughter, Dad!" she reminded him.

"That doesn't mean you're not still my favorite," he joked.

Megan smiled. She was glad that her father was in a good mood. "Are you still working on that news article about the peace talks in Africa?" she asked.

"I sure am," Mr. Ryder replied. "But not for long! The government has just agreed to the reforms the revolutionaries have been fighting for. It looks as if the war here may really be over."

"That's great." I'm so glad Dad always tells me exactly what's happening wherever he is, no matter how scary or complicated it is, Megan thought. Some adults wouldn't think a ten-year-old was mature enough to know the truth. But he understands that I'd be even more worried about him if I didn't know where he was or what he was doing. "That's great!" she said again as his words began to sink in.

"It is," Mr. Ryder agreed. "It's great because the people here aren't fighting with each other any more. It's also great because it means I can head back to the States and see my favorite daughter very soon."

"Really?" Megan was thrilled. Oh, please, be here Saturday, she silently pleaded. Please, Dad. She crossed her fingers. "How soon?"

"Friday—day after tomorrow," Mr. Ryder said. "I'll be there for Father-Daughter Day at your camp."

"You remembered!" Megan cried happily.

"Of course I remembered," her father said with a laugh. Megan wasn't really surprised. Being a foreign news correspondent kept her father very busy, but not too busy to remember important things. "I already booked my flight. I wanted to be sure I'll get there in plenty of time," Mr. Ryder went on. "I'd better hang up now, Megan, but I'll see you in two days. Okay?"

"Okay. I can't wait," Megan said. "Bye, Dad! Have a nice flight home."

Megan was just hanging up the phone when the doorbell rang. "I'll get it!" she sang out to Aunt Frances, who was in the living room reading her favorite rock-climbing magazine. "It's probably my friends."

Megan skipped to the front door, feeling lighthearted and happy. When she threw open the door, she saw her best friends—Alison McCann, Heather Hardin, Rose Hopkins, and Keisha Vance—standing on the wide, shady front porch.

"Come on in," she greeted them cheerfully. "I've got big news!"

"What is it?" Alison asked, immediately curious.

"Upstairs," Megan invited, leading the way. "Come on!"

An Exciting Phone Call

Soon all five of the girls were gathered in Megan's large, comfortable bedroom. Alison sprawled on the bed, her blond ponytail trailing on the stenciled coverlet. Across the room, Keisha was poking around the contents of Megan's bookshelves. Ginger had seated herself on Rose's lap as soon as she sat down in the overstuffed chair near the window. Ginger purred contentedly as she scratched the cat's head. Heather was sitting cross-legged on the cozy green rug near the bed. Megan herself sat in her desk chair, turning it around to face the room.

"Guess what?" she told her friends excitedly. "My dad's definitely going to make it to Father-Daughter Day!"

"Hurray!" Alison exclaimed.

Rose nodded, tucking her long, dark hair behind one ear. "Now all our dads will be there. It's going to be so much fun!"

Heather leaned over to pat Megan on the knee. "You must be so excited to see him," she said. "I'm really happy for you."

Megan smiled, grateful to have such nice friends. She and Alison and Keisha had known one another for years. She had met Heather and Rose more recently, yet she felt as though the five of them had been best friends forever. She thought that part of the reason was the wonderful secret they all shared—the secret of their neighbor Ellie Goodwin's incredible attic. Whenever the five girls tried on any of the beautiful, exotic outfits from the old steamer trunk in the attic and gazed into the mirror, they were swept away into a thrilling adventure.

But Megan's thoughts soon turned from Ellie and her attic back to Father-Daughter Day.

"What do you think we'll be doing?" she asked her friends, her green eyes sparkling with anticipation. "On Saturday, I mean."

Alison jumped up. "I know! I asked one of the counselors today. There'll be sack races, a water balloon toss, a scavenger hunt... " She started counting things off on her fingers. "...Wheelbarrow races..."

Megan wrinkled her nose. "Wheelbarrow races?" she repeated uncertainly, imagining her father pushing her around at top speed in a dirty old garden cart.

"You know—wheelbarrow races," Keisha explained, her wide dark eyes encouraging. "That's when one partner walks on her hands while the other partner holds her legs. You know, so the first partner looks kind of like a wheelbarrow."

Megan wasn't sure she liked the sound of that. "Isn't it kind of hard to walk on your hands that way?"

"Sure!" Alison laughed. "That's what makes it so much fun. Watch!" She jumped off the bed and poked Keisha on the shoulder. "Come on, let's show her."

A moment later, Keisha and Alison were

wheelbarrowing across Megan's room. Keisha plodded about, more or less upright, holding on to Alison's sneakered feet, while Alison "stepped" forward on her arms. Ginger hopped off Rose's lap to investigate. The cat stretched, yawned, then strolled over to Alison, extending her neck to sniff her face.

Alison giggled. "Hey! Those whiskers tickle." She shook her head. Ginger stepped forward and batted gently at her nose with one paw. At that, Alison started laughing harder. Her arms shook and then buckled, and she collapsed onto the floor, almost bringing Keisha down with her.

Megan joined in as her friends burst out laughing. Secretly, though, she felt a little nervous. She wasn't as athletic as Alison or Keisha, and she didn't really like getting messy and sweaty. Some of the activities Alison had listed sounded like fun, but Megan wasn't sure she would be very good at any of them, except maybe the scavenger hunt.

"What other games do you think we'll be playing?" she asked.

"Oh, tons of stuff," Heather said. "One of the older kids said something about an obstacle course, and I bet there'll be a canoe race on the lake."

Alison nodded. "I hope so. I'm great at paddling," she bragged, plopping back onto Megan's bed and pretending it was a canoe, leaning over the side to use an imaginary paddle.

"Oh yeah?" Heather challenged, a twinkle in her brown eyes. "You'd better watch out. My father was on the rowing team in college."

Alison grinned. "Well, you and your dad had better watch out," she said. "If you get too close, I might have to tip you into the water."

Megan smiled as her friends joked around with one another. Inside, though, she was still worried. Some of her enthusiasm for Father-Daughter Day had faded when she heard the list of activities. Somehow, she realized, she hadn't really thought about exactly what they would all be doing. She had just imagined how much fun it would be to spend the day with her dad and her friends at day camp.

Still, she reminded herself, that part was still true. No matter what activities were scheduled, at least her father would be there to help her. That thought made her feel better. Her dad wouldn't make her do anything she didn't want to do. She could trust him.

Chapter

Two

AUNT FRANCES STEPS IN

 ear Diary,
Happy Thursday! I'm so
excited that Dad is coming home
tomorrow! When I talked to him on the
phone yesterday, he sounded as if he's
really looking forward to Father-Daughter
Day. I am, too, even though I'm still not sure
about being in the wheelbarrow—

"Megan! Megan, can you come down

here for a moment, please?"

Megan frowned, annoyed at being interrupted in the middle of a thought. But she set her pen down and hopped off the bed.

"Coming!" she yelled to Aunt Frances. She found her aunt standing at the bottom of the stairs.

"Come sit down with me, Megs," Aunt Frances said, turning and heading into the living room. "I have to tell you something."

"Was that Mom on the phone?" Megan asked, hoping her mother wouldn't have to work late again. Then she remembered… "She's not sick, is she? She wasn't feeling very well this morn—"

Aunt Frances held up one hand to hush her. "Everyone's fine," she assured Megan. She sat down on the sofa and patted the space beside her. "And that wasn't your mom on the phone. It was your dad."

"Dad called again?" Megan glanced toward the phone as she sank onto the sofa next to her aunt. "Why didn't I get to talk to him?"

Aunt Frances sighed. Worry lines creased her normally cheerful face.

"He only had a few seconds to talk," she explained gently. "You see, more fighting has broken out over there. The treaty he told you about yesterday is in jeopardy. He has to stay until they work out these new problems."

Megan felt her stomach clench. She couldn't believe her ears. "I don't understand," she cried. "I thought the war was over."

Aunt Frances sighed. "I thought so, too, Megs. Everyone did."

"But Dad was supposed to come home tomorrow," Megan insisted, feeling her eyes fill with tears. She did her best not to let them spill over, not wanting to look like a baby. "He was supposed to be here tomorrow."

"I know, honey." Aunt Frances gave her a sympathetic look and rubbed her shoulder comfortingly. "I'm sorry.

But there's no way he could have predicted this." She leaned over and picked up the TV remote control. Pushing a button, she brought the television in the corner of the room to life. Then she quickly switched to the all-news channel. "Let's watch the news coverage, okay? Maybe we can get some answers that way."

Megan stared at the screen at the reporter who was talking about the fighting and the failed peace treaty. Her head was spinning as she watched the thick, dark smoke pouring from burning buildings, angry people running and shouting, soldiers with guns. It was horrible.

Why did Dad and Mom have to get divorced, anyway? Megan thought helplessly. If they were still married, Mom might be home already. Maybe Dad would be right here in the living room, safe, watching TV with her, instead of far, far away in the middle of a war. Maybe—

Then she shook her head and sighed. She knew that her parents would love their jobs just as much even if they had stayed married. Dad had traveled a lot even when he lived here with them. But at times like this it was hard to remember that.

"Why do people have to fight, anyway?" she complained bitterly. "There shouldn't be any wars." Or any divorces, she thought, though she didn't say it.

"I agree," Aunt Frances said quietly. She sighed and turned to face Megan. "But sometimes people feel they have to fight for something they believe in. For instance, those people, the revolutionaries," she gestured at the television, "are fighting their government for the same kinds of rights you and I take for granted. Safety for their families. Freedom. Respect."

"I wish they'd find a different way to get them," Megan muttered, crossing her arms across her chest.

"I know. But plenty of people are working hard to get the two sides negotiating again. That's where your dad is, not where there's shooting now."

Megan just shrugged. She knew her aunt was trying to help, but it wasn't making Megan feel much better. She wouldn't feel better until her father was home again—safe and sound.

"Oh well," she said with a sigh. "I guess this means Father-Daughter Day is ruined." She bit her lip, once again feeling as though she might start to cry. "I'll probably just stay home. The counselors said we could bring our mothers instead, but Mom already told me she has an important meeting on Saturday."

Megan was secretly glad about that. Not having her father show up for Father-Daughter Day was bad enough. Having her mother come instead would be downright embarrassing—especially since all her friends' fathers were going. Megan didn't mind standing out from the crowd when it was because she said something interesting or did well on a test or won a board game. But she didn't like being different in certain other ways, such as having divorced parents, or messing up in gym class— or going someplace with her mother when all the other kids were with their fathers.

Aunt Frances smiled and pressed the power button to turn off the TV.

"Hey, don't worry about that, Megs," she exclaimed. "You don't have to miss the big day. I'd be happy to be your partner!"

"You?" Megan said uncertainly. "Um,...are you sure that's a good idea?"

"Of course!" Aunt Frances replied cheerfully. "It'll be fun." She leaned over and patted Megan fondly on the knee. "We'll be an unbeatable team. Those other folks won't know what hit them!"

Megan smiled weakly, not knowing what to say. It's supposed to be *Father*-Daughter Day, she thought unhappily. Not Mother-Daughter Day. And definitely not *Aunt-Niece* Day! There was no way she could show up with Aunt Frances as her partner. She couldn't do it—she just couldn't. It would be too embarrassing.

But how could she tell Aunt Frances she didn't want her to come?

C h a p t e r
Three

INTO THE AMAZON

egan quickly excused herself. If her father couldn't come to Father-Daughter Day, she didn't want anyone to come. Aunt Frances could be a lot of fun, but she could also be…well, a little too enthusiastic, too loud, too different. Nobody at day camp would be able to miss the fact that Megan's father wasn't there. They'd all end up feeling sorry for her, and it would be totally humiliating.

She went up to her room and shut the door. Her diary

was still on the bed where she'd left it. Megan picked up her pen.

Dear Diary, she wrote. I just got some ~~terribel~~ terrible news! Some stupid people are having a war, so Dad ~~is~~ can't come home from ~~Affr~~ Africa yet, and so now ~~there~~ I mean I—

She couldn't seem to concentrate long enough to write a proper sentence. She was so upset that she couldn't even spell correctly, even though she was usually the best speller in her whole class. Megan angrily threw her pen across the room. Ginger pounced on it and whacked it under the desk.

She couldn't talk to her friends about this. None of their parents were divorced, and all of their fathers were going on Saturday. Even Heather's dad had arranged his flight schedule so he could be there.

It's not fair, Megan thought. Why can't I have a normal family like my friends do?

She sighed and pulled at her bangs, feeling sad and angry and hopeless all at the same time.

"I think I need to distract myself, Ginger." Megan addressed the cat, but she was really talking to herself. Maybe later, when her mother got home, Megan would talk to her about what to do. In the meantime, the best thing she could do was to try not to think about it too much.

Luckily, she knew of one surefire distraction. It was

almost guaranteed to take her mind off everything else. She would go to Ellie's attic.

"Thanks a lot," Megan called over her shoulder as she headed up the stairs to the second floor of Ellie's spacious Victorian house, the golden key clutched in her hand.

In the attic, she headed straight for the old steamer trunk, lifted the lid, and closed her eyes. "I want to find something really different," she murmured as she plunged in her hands.

She pulled out khaki shorts and a shirt with bright parrots and lizards against a background of tropical leaves. Socks and a deep yellow neck scarf were stuffed inside the hiking boots. Megan stared at them uncertainly. It wasn't quite what she had expected to find.

She was about to put the clothes back and try again. But then she hesitated.

"Why not?" she whispered, quickly kicking off her shoes and changing into the new outfit. "I wanted something different."

She settled the matching hat firmly on her head and looked down at herself. Let's see how I look, she thought, and walked over to the mirror. Despite her doubts, she

liked what she saw.

"Neat," she said aloud, speaking to her own reflection. "I look pretty adventurous, don't I?"

"What? Did you say something?" a girl's voice demanded from just behind her.

Megan whirled around. Instead of the high dormer windows at the far end of the attic, her gaze met huge tree trunks covered with twining vines. The attic had been cool and dry; now the air she breathed was moist, heavy, and hot. When she moved her arms, it almost felt as if she were moving them through water instead of air. Smells of sweet and spicy flowers, damp ground, and fresh leaves filled her nose. Sounds of unfamiliar bird calls and running water surrounded her.

Megan gasped. She had never been here before, but she immediately guessed where she was. "It's a rain forest!" she whispered in awe.

The voice came again. "What did you say, Megan? Are you talking to yourself or something?"

Megan turned her head and saw a girl about her own age standing beside her. The girl was a little taller than Megan herself, with a dark blond ponytail and a tanned face. She was wearing an outfit very similar to Megan's.

"Uh, no, I didn't say anything," Megan said quickly. "Sorry."

The other girl rolled her eyes. "Hey, it's okay," she said. Her voice was loud and rather grumpy. "I talk to myself sometimes, too. Just this morning I asked myself, 'Hey Dana, do you think your mom and dad are ever going to come to their senses and move back to America? Or are we going to be stuck in this stupid Amazon rain forest forever?'"

Megan's breath caught in her throat and her eyes went wide.

I can't believe it, she thought in amazement, looking around once again. I'm really here—in the Amazon rain forest!

Chapter

Four

THE BOREALIS BUTTERFLY

o, anyway," Dana went on, "I'm glad our parents are friends and that yours let you come visit. I've hardly talked to any other Americans since we moved here last year." She rolled her eyes. "Except my parents and the other scientists, I mean. And they don't count. They're always trying to get me interested in their latest discoveries and junk like that. They don't even care that I'm bored stiff out here in the stupid jungle." She sighed. "I mean, there are no swimming pools or movie theaters anywhere around. There aren't even any radio or TV shows in English, except for boring grownup stuff on the shortwave radio. Nothing to do except look at a bunch of ugly plants and gross bugs and snakes."

While Dana was speaking, a flash of color caught Megan's eye. She turned just in time to see a large red and green parrot dart through the air nearby. Before she could get a good look, the beautiful bird was gone, hidden again in the dense forest. But many other birds—some large, some small, most brightly colored— chirped and cawed and twittered from every direction. Megan hardly knew where to look first.

Only a couple of months earlier, Megan had done a school research report on the Amazon rain forest. She loved anything having to do with animals or nature, and she had found the assignment so interesting that she had written ten whole pages. She'd gotten an A+ from her teacher. Now she was here in person, seeing and hearing and even smelling the very things she had studied!

She was grateful for her good memory as she thought back to the facts and figures she had included in her report. Glancing around, she noticed the many dark green, leafy plants growing nearby on the forest floor. She even recognized one or two kinds of plants from home—they looked like some of the houseplants her aunt liked to raise in the family's sunny dining room. Megan had read that this lowest section of the rain forest was usually called the understory, and that it received only a little bit of light from the sun. Now, looking around, she saw that this was very true. It was quite dim where she and Dana were standing with only dappled bits of sunlight peeping through.

Looking upward, Megan saw a thick jumble of leaves, vines, and branches above her. That was the reason very little light made it through to the understory—the canopy layer of the forest.

When she looked down again, Dana was crouched on the ground nearby, digging through her backpack. "What are you doing?" Megan asked.

"I'm looking for that picture I promised to show you as soon as we got far enough away from the village," Dana mumbled, distracted by her search. "I know it's in here somewhere."

Megan had no idea what the other girl was talking about, but she figured she would find out soon enough. In the meantime, she was still a little overwhelmed at being in the rain forest. To settle herself down, she tried to think

of other things she had learned from writing her report.

"Did you know there's more than one type of rain forest?" she said. Without waiting for Dana to answer, she went on. "The Amazon is an equatorial one. That means it's near the equator in the tropics. Did you know that more than half the species of animals and plants in the whole world live in rain forests?"

Dana sniffed and glanced up at her. "You sound like my parents," she said, rather sourly. "They're always talking about stuff like that. How important the rain forest is, blah blah blah. That's why they insisted we move here, even though I told them a million times I didn't want to."

"They're right about it being important," Megan said, more than a little surprised at the other girl's attitude. Sure, moving away from home must be kind of tough. But, to Megan, living in the rain forest seemed like a really neat opportunity.

"Aha!" Dana cried suddenly. She straightened up, a piece of paper clutched in her hand. "Here it is." She shoved the paper toward Megan. It seemed to be a page torn from a magazine, containing a large photograph of a butterfly and a short article underneath.

"Wow," Megan exclaimed as she looked at the picture. "It's gorgeous!" The butterfly's large, graceful wings were a rainbow of emerald green, vibrant red, glorious purple, sunny yellow and bright turquoise blue. Its slender body and long antennae were almost black with colored markings that matched the wings.

Dana grinned. "That's a borealis butterfly," she said. "I want to find them. There are supposed to be some in this section of the forest somewhere. But no one—not even my brilliant scientist parents—has seen one in years." She shrugged. "They're supposed to be really rare or something."

Megan nodded. She knew that many of the plants, animals, and insects in the rain forest were endangered.

That meant there were only a few of them left. She wondered whether the borealis butterfly was one of those species.

She couldn't help feeling surprised that Dana seemed so excited about a butterfly. She had started to think that Dana wasn't interested in anything about the rain forest. Maybe she's not such a grump after all, Megan thought with a secret smile. Then again, maybe she just wanted to help her parents with their work so they could all go home sooner.

Either way, Megan was eager to help. She quickly scanned the article beneath the photograph. It explained that the borealis butterfly liked to live near bodies of still water in thick underbrush, and that they were especially active just after a heavy rainfall.

Dana took the picture back, folded it carefully, and stuck it back in her pack. "My parents told me you're pretty smart, so I thought you could help."

"Sure!" It would be fun to search for the beautiful borealis butterflies—sort of like a mystery. Megan loved solving mysteries, even if she usually only found them in the books she read. A real mystery, especially one that involved an interesting animal, was even more exciting. Besides, it sounded as though they would be helping Dana's parents and the other scientists a lot if they found the butterflies. They might even be helping to save an endangered species! "Let's get started," Megan said eagerly. She tried to think of the best way to start their search. "Do you know of any bodies of water around here?"

"The river is really close, " Dana replied. "Hear it? That's where I've been looking for the butterflies so far. Come on." She started off to their right.

Megan thought back to what the article had said. "No, wait," she said, hurrying after Dana. "A river can't be the right place—it's running water. The article said borealises only like still water, remember?"

"Really?" Dana dug out the article once again. She unfolded it and looked at it carefully. "Hey, you're right," she said. She thought for a moment. "One of the kids in the village said something about a big pool of water over that way." She waved to the west. "He said there were piranhas in it, though, so nobody ever swims in it, and the adults don't even know it's there." She shrugged. "I thought he was just trying to scare me, but maybe it's for real. Anyway, he told me where it is. I bet we can find it."

"Okay, let's go." Megan nodded.

The two girls walked deeper into the forest, moving slowly because of the plants, fallen tree trunks, and rocks in their way. Megan heard chattering noises from somewhere above their heads. She looked up and saw a group of at least twenty lithe, quick-moving creatures high among the branches. It was hard to get an accurate count of how many there were, since the monkeys were continually swinging from branch to branch or vine to vine, popping out from behind clumps of leaves and trunks of taller trees.

"Look at that!" Megan was so excited that her voice shook a little. She pointed as Dana stopped and glanced upward. "See? I'm pretty sure those are spider monkeys. I've read about them—they like to hang out in the middle level of the forest canopy. That one is hanging by its tail—isn't that neat? Their tails are sort of like an extra arm. Tails like that are called prehensile, and only certain species of monkeys have them." Megan was proud of herself for remembering the difficult word.

Dana rolled her eyes. "Big deal," she muttered. "We're

supposed to be looking for butterflies, not monkeys, remember? Besides, I can look at monkeys in the zoo back home."

"But that isn't the same as seeing them in their natural home." Megan really didn't understand why Dana wasn't more excited about being here. Before she could ask her about it, she felt a splash on the end of her nose. She looked up again. "Hey, it's raining."

Dana laughed. "Of course," she said sarcastically. "It's a *rain* forest, remember? It rains here all the time." She snorted. "That's one more reason I wish my parents had decided to stay at home—where it's dry."

Within seconds, the rain was coming down in sheets. Megan was soaked before she could even get her poncho out of her pack. But she didn't care. This was perfect. If they could find the pool by the time the rain stopped, and if borealis butterflies did live there, they would be much more likely to spot the rare species.

"Come on," she told Dana, more excited than ever. "Let's hurry!"

chapter Five

A Horrible Plan

he and Dana fought their way through the underbrush and trees for almost an hour. Several times, after checking Dana's compass, they'd had to backtrack some and start again. The farther they went, the narrower and more overgrown the path became. Before long, the girls had found themselves ducking under branches, pushing aside vines and leaves, and even dodging large, intricately woven spider webs stretched across the path.

"Are you sure this is the right way?" Megan asked, panting as she jumped over a fallen log. She paused to catch her breath and wait for Dana to catch up.

Dana looked around uncertainly. "Sure I'm sure," she said, sounding more confident than she looked.

Megan sighed and looked up. It was still raining, but the downpour was a lot lighter now. "Come on, let's hurry," she urged. "We have to find that side path before the rain stops."

"Go ahead," Dana said, puffing with exertion. "I'm right behind you."

Megan started forward, anxiously scanning both sides of the trail, then stopped again. Something was tugging at her sleeve. As she turned to untangle the slender vine that had caught in her shirt, she saw an enormous macaw sitting on a low branch. And something else. Megan stared.

"Dana, look! The trail branches off here. Do you think…?"

"Finally!" Dana said in an exasperated tone. "Let's go!"

Moments later, the two girls emerged from the trees, just in time to watch the last drops of rain splash into the rippling, dark surface of a large, deep pool.

"Wow!" Megan whispered under her breath as she stared about her. The entire area was walled in by thick vegetation, and even the sounds of the forest seemed distant and subdued in this hidden place.

"This just has to be the place," Dana said. "So, where are the butterflies?"

"Ssshhh," said Megan, and crept forward to perch on a boulder.

While the girls watched for movement among the leaves, the sun came out, beaming down through the opening in the canopy just above the water. After a quarter hour, Dana began to shift around impatiently, talking about looking for another pool.

Megan thought she saw a flash of color out of the corner of her eye.

"Look!" she cried. "Over there." By the time the words were out of her mouth, whatever it was had disappeared.

Both girls peered eagerly toward the spot where Megan had seen the movement. A moment later, two colorful creatures fluttered out of a tangle of vines.

"Look!" Megan gasped, pointing. "Over there!"

"I think that's them!" Dana whispered excitedly.

Dana grabbed the binoculars out of her pack and peered through them, carefully bringing one of the butterflies into sharp focus. She could see every splash of color on its

wings, each slender leg and antenna. It looked exactly like the butterfly in the magazine.

"I think they are," Megan agreed. She glanced around. "It makes sense," she pointed out. "This is exactly the kind of habitat your article said they like." As the words left her mouth, several butterflies drifted into view.

She and Dana watched silently for a few minutes. More and more borealis butterflies appeared, fluttering out over the water and drifting over the girls' heads. It was a beautiful sight—dozens of brightly colored butterflies dancing on the warm breeze like airborne jewels or tiny rainbows. Megan thought she had never seen anything so magical in her life.

"This is terrific," Dana said, sounding impressed. "I can't believe my parents never found this place. But they hardly ever come in this direction. They don't know what they're missing!"

"Isn't it wonderful?" Megan agreed breathlessly, her eyes on a particularly large and brightly colored butterfly that had just landed on the palm of her outstretched hand.

Dana nodded. "I never would have found it without you," she admitted. "I forgot about the 'still water' part. I guess that explains why I never had any luck looking for these guys by the river."

With that, she bent over and started digging around in

her backpack again. She pulled a large glass jar out and grinned with anticipation.

"What's that for?" Megan asked.

Dana unscrewed the metal lid. "What do you think?" she asked. "It's to catch one of the butterflies."

Megan blinked, not understanding for a moment. Then her eyes widened. "But—but there are no air holes in the lid!" she sputtered.

"No kidding," Dana muttered. She wasn't really paying much attention to Megan. Holding the lid in one hand and the jar in the other, she glanced around.

"But if you put a butterfly in there, it will die," Megan protested, horrified. She couldn't believe this. Was Dana planning to kill one of these beautiful insects?

Dana glanced at her, looking annoyed. "No kidding," she said again in a sarcastic tone. "It would be pretty hard to pin a *live* butterfly to a card."

"But I thought—I thought we were just looking for their habitat so we could tell your parents about it," Megan exclaimed.

Dana snorted. "My parents?" she said. "Get real. Why would I help them? They're the reason I'm stuck here, miles and miles away from my friends and my real home."

She shook her head. "Nope. I figure, if I've got to be here, I might as well try to fit in. The village kids will definitely be impressed if they see that I've caught one of these." She gestured toward the butterflies that were still flying all around them.

"But why do you have to kill it?" Megan cried. "Why not just capture one, show it to the other kids, then let it go? I mean, you said they're rare—they might even be endangered. You're not supposed to kill endangered animals!"

Dana shrugged, looking stubborn. "A butterfly isn't really an animal. It's a bug," she said. "Besides, what difference will one measly butterfly make? It's not like I'm going to take all of them." Her eyes lit up when she noticed the extra-large borealis, which was still perched nearby, moving its wings slowly up and down. "Ha," she muttered. "That looks like a good one."

Dana slowly crept forward, step by step, trying not to disturb the beautiful butterfly until she got close enough to nab it.

Megan didn't know what to do. "Just think about it a little more," she urged desperately. "Are you sure you want to do this? It's not right."

Dana ignored her. She moved forward another step, and then another. Finally, she was almost within reach of the unsuspecting butterfly.

"That's right," she murmured, inching the jar toward the twig where the creature sat. "Hold still. Just another minute...."

Chapter

Six

MEGAN'S IDEA

egan's mind was moving at triple speed. She couldn't just stand here and let Dana destroy an innocent living thing. But how could she stop her?

Maybe she could grab the jar out of her hand. She could probably sneak up and surprise her. She and Dana were about the same size, and Dana wouldn't be expecting her to do anything like that. Should she trip Dana? No, Megan knew she could never do it. It would be too much like actually attacking Dana. She might fall onto one of these rocks at the edge of the pool and get hurt. Even the thought made Megan shudder.

If she wanted to save the butterfly, she had to think of something else—and fast. What about waving her arms and scaring the butterfly away? No, that would make Dana mad, and it wouldn't really solve the problem—she could always come back another time, when Megan wasn't with her.

"That's right," Dana crooned, moving her jar still closer to the large borealis. "Don't be scared."

Megan's breath caught in her throat as the butterfly moved its wings a little faster. Fly! she thought urgently. Fly away!

Instead, it fluttered and hopped a short distance— landing right on the lip of Dana's jar!

"Wait!" Megan cried loudly. She just needed a little more time to think. "Don't move!"

Dana froze, a surprised look on her face.

"What is it?" she asked. She sounded a little frightened. "Is there a snake?" Her hands shook—just enough to dislodge the butterfly from her jar. It fluttered upward and disappeared into the leaves nearby.

Megan let out a breath of relief. But she knew this wasn't over. That butterfly might have escaped, but there were still plenty of others flying around the pool. If she didn't talk Dana out of her plan, she would simply

capture a different one.

"There's no snake," she said. "I just want to talk to you."

Dana looked disgusted. She shook the jar at Megan.

"Are you crazy?" she complained. "That was probably the hugest butterfly around here. And, thanks to you, it got away!" She looked around and sighed. "Oh, well. I can find another one, or maybe get two smaller ones instead. That would still look pretty good."

"Wait!" Megan cried again. "Just listen to me for a second, okay?"

"Why should I?" Dana snapped.

Megan felt her own hands start to shake. She didn't really like fighting with people—even when only words were involved.

"I just don't think you realize what you're doing," she said, trying to keep her voice steady and calm. "You may think it's just one butterfly so it's no big deal. But that's not really true. All the life in the rain forest—and everywhere else, too—is part of a big, connected pattern." She paused. "Different animals need other animals and plants for food or pollination or—or other things—"

"Right," Dana interrupted, sounding more annoyed than ever. "Just the way *I* happen to need one of those butterflies right now. And I'm going to get one, whether you like it or not." Then she headed toward the pond.

Megan gulped. "But if the butterflies are already endangered, it won't take much for them to become extinct. And sometimes when one species of plant or animal becomes extinct, other ones do, too— because they depended on that species." She took a deep breath and went on. "And I read once that more than thirty species become extinct every day in tropical rain forests all over the world."

Dana didn't answer. Instead, she stopped and glared at Megan, then took a step toward her, scowling.

"Why don't you mind your own beeswax?" she yelled, waving one clenched fist under Megan's nose. "I don't need you telling me what to do. Besides, why should I care if a few bugs and plants become extinct?"

Megan felt her knees trembling a little. If she kept on, Dana might start a real fight. Then what would Megan do?

"You can yell at me all you want," she told Dana firmly. "But what I'm saying is true. And you should care just as much as I do. Because every living thing depends on other living things for life, including humans. If too many other species become extinct, people might become extinct someday, too."

Dana paused. She seemed to be thinking about what Megan had said. But after a moment, she shrugged.

"So what?" she muttered. "It's just one butterfly. And I need it to make the other kids like me." Still, she didn't sound quite as sure as she had before.

Megan knew that this was her chance—she had to convince Dana once and for all, now that she was actually listening.

Suddenly it came to her. The perfect plan!

"I know a better way to make people like you, Dana,"

she said eagerly. "Instead of capturing a butterfly, why don't you show your parents this place? Then, they can study the butterflies and maybe learn important things from them—things that could help people all over the world. And it'll all be thanks to you!"

"I don't know," Dana said, still looking doubtful. "I wanted to show the other kids. You just got here, Megan. You don't know how awful it's been."

"Come on!" Megan urged. "The village kids will still know that you were the one who found the butterflies. They'll probably be even more impressed if you show them lots of *live* ones than if you just have one *dead* one." She hesitated. "Besides," she added reluctantly, "if that doesn't work, you can always come back here, now that you know where the butterflies are." She held her breath, waiting for Dana to make up her mind.

"All right," Dana said after a moment. "I guess I could try it your way first. What have I got to lose?"

C h a p t e r
Seven

MEGAN'S PLAN

a! Daddy!" Dana shouted, yanking open the flimsy metal door on a large trailer. "Are you in here?"

Megan hung back, playing nervously with her compass, while Dana stuck her head through the door. Dana had already told her that this trailer was where her parents and the other scientists had their office. A couple of backpacks, a pup tent, and some folding canvas chairs were just outside the trailer, along with equipment that

Megan didn't recognize.

"Dana?" a woman's voice replied from inside. "You sound excited. What's going on?"

Dana waved at Megan. "Come on in," she said, "so we can tell them."

Megan stepped up into the trailer and looked around. The long, narrow space had been turned into a combination laboratory, storage area, and library. Scientific books and pamphlets lined the walls at one end. A metal shelving unit groaned under the weight of more books, piles of paper, and jars and vials and boxes filled with all sorts of things. A couple of large white tables held test tubes, scientific-looking equipment, and two computers.

Megan hardly had time to take it all in before she found herself being introduced to Dana's parents and three other scientists. None of them looked the way she expected. She had pictured scientists as older, stern-looking people who wore white lab coats and spent their time peering into microscopes. Except for a large microscope among the other equipment, Megan's ideas were nowhere near the truth. Only one of the scientists was over fifty, perhaps around Ellie's age. The other four were much younger. Instead of wearing lab coats, they were dressed in jeans or khaki shorts a lot like Megan's and Dana's. And they looked friendly and welcoming, not

stern at all.

"Megan thought I should tell you," Dana said to her mother, a tall woman with a clipboard in one hand. "We saw something today. Um…we found some borealis butterflies."

Dana's mother grabbed Dana's hands. "Oh, Dana!" she cried excitedly.

"Are you certain?" the older scientist asked, hurrying forward from her seat at one of the computers. "A lot of butterflies look alike, you know."

Megan nodded. "We're pretty sure," she said. "Dana has a photograph from a magazine. The butterflies looked just like the one in the picture." She felt a little nervous— adults didn't always believe what kids told them, especially when it came to things such as this. But the scientists were already heading for the door, grabbing hats, cameras, and other equipment as they went.

"You've got to show us!" Dana's father said, banging his beaker onto the table in his excitement. He grabbed a backpack off a hook behind the door and slung it over his shoulder.

They all left the trailer and followed Dana and Megan into the forest. One dark-skinned young woman with wild, curly hair nodded and rubbed her hands together as she walked.

"This is exciting news," she said. "The villagers kept

telling me these butterflies still exist, but I thought they were making it up just to please us. I was sure the borealis must be extinct. However did you girls find them?"

Megan opened her mouth to explain how she had figured out where to look, but she thought better of it.

"Dana did most of the work," she said instead. "She brought the article, and she knew where the pool was."

Dana shot her a surprised look. Then she smiled gratefully. "Megan helped, too," she put in.

The adults weren't really listening. They were busy chattering among themselves as the group slowly made its way through the trees.

Megan pushed aside a vine. "I hope the butterflies are still flying around," she told Dana quietly. "It's been a while since the rain stopped."

Dana cast a worried glance at her parents. "If they don't see the butterflies themselves, they won't believe we saw them, either."

Megan bit her lip. She wasn't sure that was true—after all, everyone seemed perfectly willing to believe them so far. But the important thing was what Dana thought.

"Don't worry, they'll still be there," Megan said, crossing her fingers behind her back for luck.

A few minutes later, the group emerged into the clearing.

"Oh, no," Dana moaned. All the beautiful multicolored

butterflies had disappeared!

The adults were looking around with interest. "I've never been to this spot before," said the curly-haired woman. "It's lovely."

A tall, thin man with a red mustache peered into the underbrush nearby. "Hmm. This seems a likely spot for the borealis, all right," he said.

Megan smiled proudly, glad that she and Dana had figured that out. "There were lots of them here before," she told the scientists. "Really. They all came out after the rain." She glanced at Dana—and fell silent. Dana had a disappointed scowl on her face. If they didn't see a butterfly, would she give up? Would she sneak back here after the next rain with her collection jar? Would she—

"There!" Dana cried suddenly. She pointed across the pool. "Look, right over there!"

Megan looked, along with everyone else. Brightly colored wings fluttered just above the water. "It's a butterfly!" she exclaimed happily. "Do you see it?"

Everyone was talking at once. The adults sounded just as excited as Megan felt—especially when Dana's mother spotted two more

borealis butterflies resting on a branch on their side of the pool. Two of the scientists pulled out cameras and crept closer to snap pictures, while another opened a notebook and started scribbling notes.

"Congratulations, girls," Dana's father said, beaming at his daughter and Megan. "This is truly an impressive discovery! You should be proud of yourselves."

"Thanks, Daddy," Dana said, grinning back at him.

Megan smiled, relieved. Her plan had worked after all!

And then she looked at Dana's mother. To her horror, she saw that the scientist was pulling a large jar out of her husband's backpack.

"Wh-what are you doing?" she asked.

Dana's mother smiled at her. "I'm going to try to capture one of the butterflies," she explained cheerfully, unscrewing the lid from the jar.

Megan felt her heart freeze. "But why?" she blurted. "You can't kill them!"

Dana's mother stared at Megan. "Oh, my dear!" she cried. "Of course not! Even if the borealis weren't a protected species, I wouldn't kill them." She held the lid where Megan could easily see the air holes in it. "We just want to capture a few so we can study them. That will allow us to learn more about the species and how to save it."

"Oh." Megan felt a little foolish for jumping to the

wrong conclusion. She watched in silence as the scientists captured several borealis butterflies from nearby branches, using butterfly nets. She swallowed hard when she saw the beautiful creatures fluttering inside the nets, and for a moment she regretted bringing these people here. Even if they hadn't killed any butterflies, they had taken away their freedom.

Then she reminded herself that the scientists needed to know more about borealises before they could save them.

Megan joined the group at the edge of the pool. Dana's father and one of the other scientists were taking measurements at the water's edge. Dana was busy looking over their shoulders, asking question after question about what they were doing. Her father answered every question patiently, looking pleased at her sudden curiosity.

Megan felt a happy smile spread across her face. Dana seems pretty interested in the rain forest all of a sudden, she thought. Won't she be surprised if she ends up becoming a nature scientist someday? It could happen.

She and her parents might even work together.

Thinking about Dana's parents reminded her of her own family. With a sigh, she admitted to herself that it was time to go back.

"Good-bye, Amazon," she whispered. Nobody heard her. Everyone was gathered around Dana, asking questions about how she had found this place. Megan backed into some thicker brush beside the water. A butterfly fluttered lazily away at her approach. She quietly pushed aside some leaves and branches and spotted a bright green tree frog clinging to a trunk only a few feet away, right next to a beautiful orchid plant with lovely flowers. As Megan inhaled the coconut-like scent, a bird darted past just above her head. And in the distance, she heard the howl of a monkey.

She stooped at the edge of the pool, keeping a close watch for piranhas. She didn't see any fish at all, so she leaned forward until she could see her reflection in the surface of the dark, still water.

Suddenly the light grew brighter. Megan blinked and looked up. She was back in Ellie's attic.

She sighed, missing the rain forest already. As she slowly changed back into her regular clothes and tucked the rain forest outfit back into the trunk, all her real-life problems came pouring back into her mind.

Somehow, though, they didn't seem so terrible

anymore. Megan was still worried about her father, and she knew that she would continue to worry until the war was over and he was safe at home. But now, at least she was starting to understand that some things really were worth fighting for. Hadn't she, herself, almost decided to fight Dana over killing a single butterfly?

Her problem with her aunt really wasn't very big, compared to all the serious troubles in the world. If she really wanted to, Megan knew she could work up the nerve to ask Aunt Frances not to come on Saturday. After all, she had managed to talk Dana out of catching that butterfly—and Dana was a lot bossier and scarier than Aunt Frances. But keeping Aunt Frances away just didn't seem important enough to make it worth hurting her feelings.

Megan sighed again and headed for the stairs. She turned off the light, pulled the door shut behind her, and carefully locked it with the golden key. Then she started downstairs. She had made up her mind—she would just let Aunt Frances come and hope for the best. It wasn't the perfect answer, and Megan was still afraid she would end up feeling embarrassed all day. But, it seemed like the right thing to do.

Chapter

Eight

FATHER-
DAUGHTER DAY

By the time Megan got up that
Saturday, her mother had
already left the house. As she
dressed, she found a note in one
of her sneakers:

Hi, *Sweetie! Sorry I couldn't
come to camp with you today. I
hope you and Frances have tons of
fun. I want both of you to tell me all*

about it when I get home tonight! Love, Mom

Megan smiled when she read the note. Then she tucked it in her pocket for luck. She was sure she was going to need it.

Megan's friends looked surprised when they saw her arrive with Aunt Frances instead of Mr. Ryder. She couldn't really blame them—she still hadn't had the nerve to tell anyone that her dad couldn't come.

Megan stuck her hand into the pocket of her yellow shorts, fingering the folded note inside as she tuned into the conversation around her.

"It sounds like so much fun," Alison was saying. "When you went on your first caving trip, were you scared?"

"Well—maybe a little," Aunt Frances replied. "But whenever I started to get nervous about being so far underground, I just pretended I was a worm. That helped."

Alison laughed. So did Keisha, Rose, Heather, and their fathers. Megan felt herself blushing. Why did Aunt Frances have to say such silly things? She hoped the others didn't think she was dumb.

"Attention, campers!" a counselor called. "It's time for Father-Daughter Day to begin!"

A cheer went up from the campers and their fathers—and Aunt Frances gave a piercing whistle. Megan gritted her teeth and looked at the ground. Maybe she should have pretended to have a stomach-ache and stayed home.

"Yeee-ha!" Aunt Frances yelled when the counselors started passing out large burlap sacks. Each team had to stand inside the sack together and hop to the finish line. "Sack racing was my major in college!"

Megan rolled her eyes, wishing she could disappear.

"Are you all right, Megan?" Heather asked, coming over to her. "You look kind of weird."

"I'm okay," Megan replied quickly. "I just wish my dad were here, that's all."

Heather smiled sympathetically. "I know," she said. "But at least your aunt could come in his place. She's great. She's so funny!" Just then Mr. Hardin called to her, and she hurried away. "Good luck in the race!" she called over her shoulder.

Heather obviously hadn't noticed how goofy and enthusiastic Aunt Frances was being. But Megan was sure other people had noticed.

She looked around at the crowd. Alison's dad was still talking to Aunt Frances, who was laughing loudly. Alison was standing nearby, grinning. When she noticed Megan looking at her, she skipped over.

"I almost forgot how much fun your aunt is, Megan," she declared. "She even makes a boring old sack race sound more exciting!"

One of the counselors blew his whistle.

"Racers, on your mark!" he called. Everyone ran to the starting line.

"Come on, Megs," Aunt Frances called, her eyes shining as Megan hurried toward her. She held their sack open. "Let's show 'em how it's done!"

"Okay." Megan smiled weakly and stepped in. She hopped cautiously, holding tight to the edge of the sack and being careful not to trip over the extra fabric at the bottom. After a few little hops, she felt Aunt Frances tapping her shoulder.

"Hey, kid," she said. "We'll never win this way. Let's

make like kangaroos and really jump!"

"But we might fall," Megan protested. At that moment, as if to prove her point, Alison and Mr. McCann tripped over their sack and sprawled on the ground. To Megan's surprise, they both laughed wildly and scrambled to their feet.

"See?" Aunt Frances said to Megan with a grin. "Falling's the best part!"

"Well, okay…" Megan said. That was all Aunt Frances needed to hear.

"Out of our way, everyone!" she called. "Kangaroos coming through!"

An hour later, Megan could hardly remember why she had been so embarrassed. She and Aunt Frances had come in second in the sack race, and they had done well in most of the other games as well. That was nice, especially since Megan hadn't been sure she'd be any good at the games. Plus, everyone absolutely loved Aunt Frances! Somehow, with her jokes and her enthusiasm, she managed to make all the games and activities more fun for everyone—even Megan.

First, during the three-legged race, Aunt Frances had pretended to be a pirate. She had started a splash fight after the canoe race. She had even led a sneak water-balloon attack on the day camp counselors after the balloon toss!

Now it was time for the wheelbarrow race. Megan frowned, remembering her friends' demonstration in her bedroom.

"Maybe we should sit this one out," she said.

Aunt Frances gave her a surprised look. "Really?" she said. "But why?"

Megan shrugged. "I'm not sure I'd be a very good wheelbarrow," she admitted softly, looking around to make sure nobody else was close enough to overhear.

Aunt Frances chuckled. "Is that all you're worried about?" she asked. "Well, don't worry, Megs. If you want, I'll be the barrow and you can push me." She grinned and winked. "Wheelbarrow racing was my minor in college."

Megan grinned back gratefully. "Okay," she agreed. "Let's go!" They got into position, and at the starter's whistle, the race was on!

At first Megan had trouble holding onto her "wheelbarrow". But once she got a good grip on her aunt's ankles, it was easy. Aunt Frances moved her arms smoothly and steadily, covering lots of ground with each step. Before she knew it, Megan was steering her over the finish line—way ahead of everyone else!

"We won!" Aunt Frances cried gleefully as she scrambled to her feet and gave Megan a hug. "We won!"

Megan grinned. "We're a pretty good team, aren't we?"

"You guys were great!" Keisha said, rubbing her shoulders. "I think I should have made my dad be the wheelbarrow—maybe we would have done better!"

"You're lucky, Megan," Alison added. "Your aunt is awesome at all of these games."

Rose nodded. "She's the best."

"Definitely," Heather put in. Megan smiled gratefully. "Do you really think so?" she asked uncertainly. "I mean, you don't think it's weird that she's here instead of my dad?"

Keisha looked surprised. "Why would we think that was weird?"

"Yeah," Heather said. "We know your dad's job is unpredictable. But just because he couldn't make it today doesn't mean you should have to miss all the fun."

"I guess you're right." Megan's smile got even bigger. "And this is fun, isn't it?"

She realized it was true. She was having fun, even though her dad wasn't there. She'd almost ruined things by asking Aunt Frances not to come. But now she was really glad she hadn't made that mistake. Megan was having the time of her life!

Diary

Dear Diary,

First of all, when I'm wrong, I'm really wrong! I thought having Aunt Frances come to Father-Daughter Day today would be the worst thing in the world. But I ended up having a great time with her, and my friends all thought she was the coolest! We even won the grand prize trophy at the end of the day. I just brought it upstairs, and right now it's sitting on the shelf above my desk where I can see it as I write this. I still wish Dad could have been there, but Aunt Frances was definitely the best substitute "dad" I could have hoped for. I'm *really* glad I changed my mind about letting her come!

The second thing I want to tell you is, I'm pretty proud of myself for standing up to

Dana—she was a lot scarier and bossier than Aunt Frances! It makes me think even more seriously about becoming a diplomat someday, like all those people working so hard to make peace over there in Africa this week.

That reminds me, Diary. There was a message from Dad on the answering machine when we got home from day camp. The negotiators and diplomats finally agreed on a deal with the revolutionaries, so everyone is happy. That means the war is really over! Dad promised to come home for a nice, long visit. He figures he'll be here early next week. He even promised to take me and my friends to the county fair next weekend to make up for missing today.

I can't wait to see him. And the fair
sounds like lots of fun. I sure hope Aunt
Frances will come with us!
Love,

Megan

LEARN MORE ABOUT IT

The borealis butterfly in this story is an imaginary species. However, there are many kinds of real butterflies that live in the Amazon Basin and the world's other rain forests, along with many other fascinating kinds of insects, animals, birds, and plants. Tropical rain forests are the richest habitat on the planet with millions of species counting on them for survival. The rain forest affects our air quality, our weather, and many other conditions the world over.

Unfortunately, the rain forest is in danger. In the middle of the twentieth century, about fifteen percent of the land on earth was covered by rain forest. Today only half of those forests remain. If this destruction isn't stopped, many more species could become extinct, weather patterns could change, and the whole world could face an environmental crisis in just a few decades.

If you want to help, you can start by learning more about the world's rain forests. Ask your parents, teachers, or librarians to help you. There are many interesting books and magazine articles about this important topic. You can also look for information on the Internet and watch for programs about the rain forest on television.